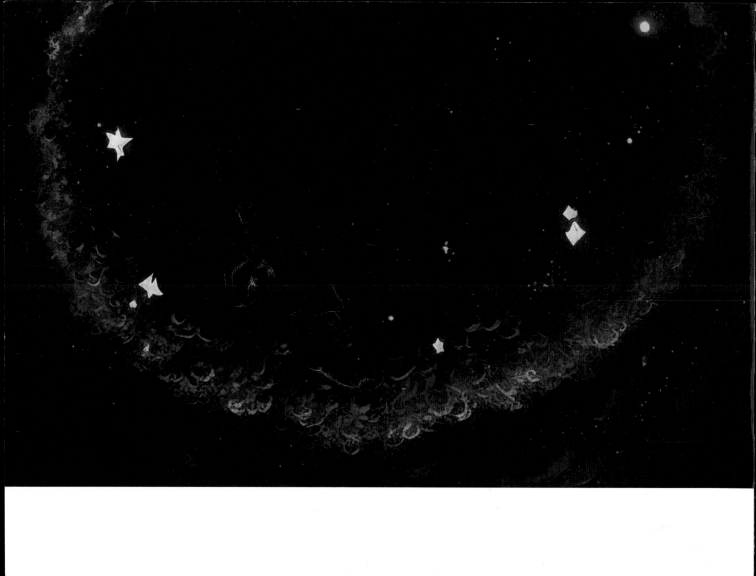

BLACK BOY, WITH DREAMS SO BOLD,
A FUTURE SO BRIGHT, YOUR STORY UNTOLD.

WITH A HEART FULL OF FIRE
AND A WILL TO SUCCEED,
YOU'LL MAKE YOUR MARK,
AND PLANT YOUR SEED.

FOR THE WORLD IS YOURS, TO EXPLORE AND TO SHAPE,
WITH YOUR TALENTS AND SKILLS, YOU'LL MAKE AN ESCAPE.

SO HOLD YOUR HEAD HIGH, AND LET YOUR LIGHT SHINE,
FOR YOU ARE A STAR, A FORCE DIVINE.

BLACK BOY, WITH A HEART OF GOLD,
YOUR POTENTIAL, IS A STORY YET TO BE TOLD.

WITH EVERY STEP,
YOU'LL LEAVE YOUR MARK,
A TRAILBLAZER,
A LEADER IN THE DARK.

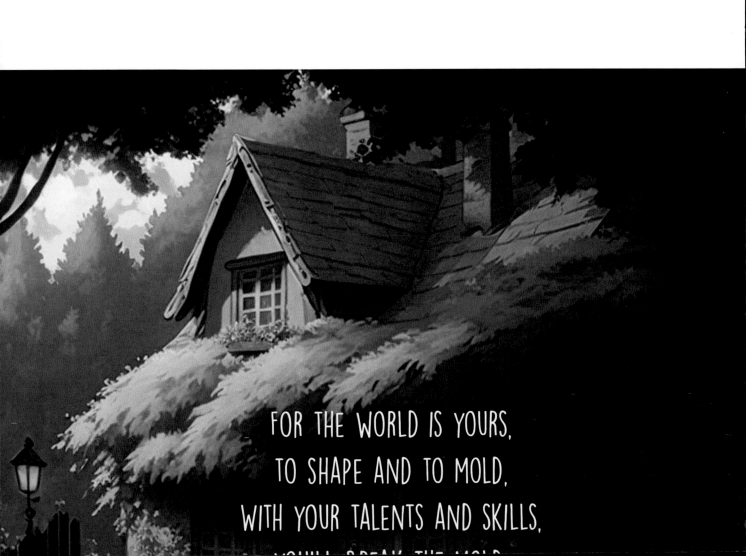

FOR THE WORLD IS YOURS,
TO SHAPE AND TO MOLD,
WITH YOUR TALENTS AND SKILLS,

YOU'LL PAVE THE WAY,
FOR THE ONES TO COME,
A SHINING EXAMPLE,
OF WHAT CAN BE DONE.

Thank you for all the love and support. I couldn't have done this without my friends or family supporting me along the way. A special thanks to Natasha Jackson and her beautiful artwork without her this wouldn't have been possible.

Their howls filled the arctic air, loud and clear, as they pulled the sleigh without any fear.

Paws strong and true, guiding the sleigh through the icy blue.

They ran and raced on a cold winter's day.

Ten little malamutes were pulling a sleigh.

Their paws pounded on the ground as they pulled the sled towards the town.

During their quest, one pup stood out from the rest. He veered right with all of his might. The wooly pup wanted to play, so he ran off to swim in the bay.

Nine little malamutes, pulling a sleigh through the snow and cold, made their way.
But on their course, one broke away and ran astray.

Eight little malamutes pulling a sleigh,
one trotted off to rest all day.

Seven little malamutes pulling a sleigh, howling their song along the way. Suddenly, they spot a herd of deer at play. One little pup ran off to chase the deer away.

Six little malamutes pulling a joyful sight,
pulling the sleigh with all of their might.

Leaving the others with the sleigh, one
ran off to skate on the lake.

Five little malamutes pulling a sleigh, exploring the winterland all day.

Through the snowy ground, one little pup heard a mouse, and with a pounce, the brave little pup started to make a cave.

Four little malamutes pulling a sleigh through the wintry forest and making their way.

Their paws leave tracks in the crisp
white snow, but one little pup leaves
the others on his own.

Three little malamutes are pulling a sleigh, kicking up powdery flurries along the way. As they ran through a clearing, the youngest pup spotted a patch of berries. He gathered them up and went on his way.

This little pup, the silliest of the pack, wanted a snack. He gathered up those berries and baked a tasty cake.

Two little malamutes pulling a sleigh,

their paws dancing on the snowy way.

Their fluffy tails held high, and they

trotted under the starry sky.

As the night grew cold, seeking
warmth and comfort from a long
day, the biggest pup ran off to hide
in some hay.

One little malamute tugged on the sleigh,
howled to her siblings

"Come back! Sit and stay!"

All ten little malamutes came running
to the call.

One by one the little malamutes
fall in line.

" **MuSHH!** " says the driver.

Then there were ten little malamutes
pulling a sleigh.

Made in the USA
Las Vegas, NV
14 December 2023